Baxter's Book

SPACE

by Leon Baxter

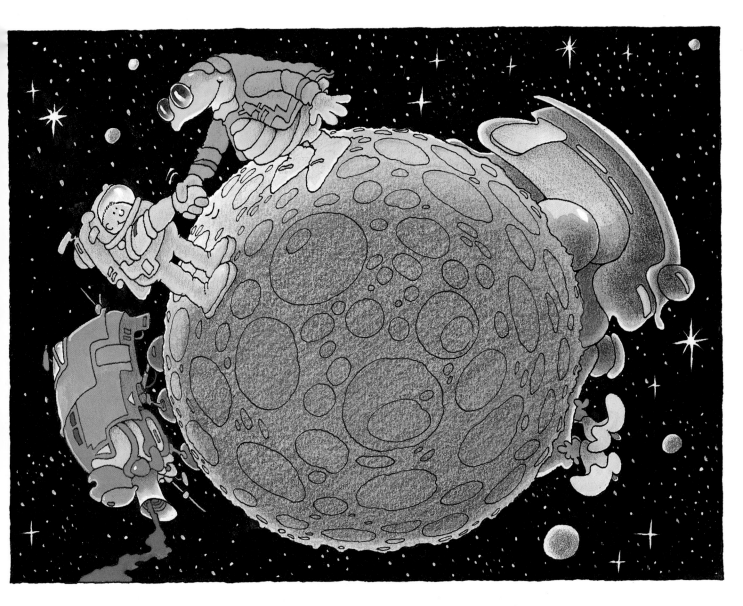

IDEALS CHILDREN'S BOOKS
Nashville, Tennessee

All about Space

This book is all about space. Space is a good subject for drawing because your imagination can go wild. Who knows what is happening far out in space? What will the future bring? Can you draw and color some space pictures of your own?

Below are some little pictures with instructions at the side. These are symbols which you will spot throughout the book. When you see them, follow their instruction.

First published in 1989 in the United States by Ideals Publishing Corp. in association with Belitha Press Limited
31 Newington Green, London N16 9PU
Text and illustrations in this format copyright © Leon Baxter 1989
Art Director: Treld Bicknell   Editor: Carol Watson
ISBN 0-8249-8377-7
Printed in Hong Kong for Imago

 Do some drawing of your own.

 Now you draw in the space provided.

 Now color the picture.

 Finish this drawing.

This is the solar system. There are nine planets and lots of asteroids and comets which revolve around a star called the sun. We live on the third planet out from the sun.

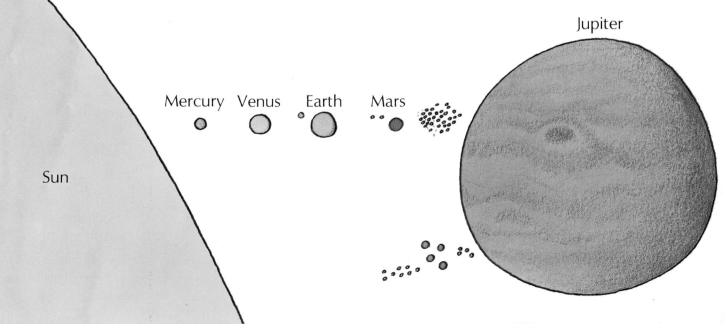

Sun

Mercury Venus Earth Mars

Jupiter

Our sun is one of millions of stars that make up the galaxy called the Milky Way.
Our galaxy is just one of millions of galaxies in the universe.
Can you paint a star picture using white paint on black paper?

The distance from the sun to the planet Pluto is more than 3.5 billion miles.
This picture shows the planets much closer together than they really are so they will all fit on
this page. If you wanted to draw an accurate scale model with the planets this size, you would
need a piece of paper over one and half miles long.

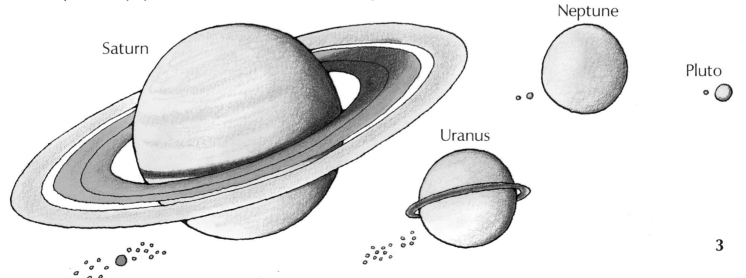

Saturn

Neptune

Pluto

Uranus

The Man in the Moon

The man in the moon is tired of people staring at him. Can you help him with some disguises?

I have given him some dark glasses and a false nose.

4

Here are some more disguises for you to use.

Can you make up your own disguises?

Robotix

These two robots have become mixed up. Can you trace or redraw them to make two separate robots?

Let's begin with
this head and body.

Space Shapes

In the earth's atmosphere cars, planes, and boats that have smooth, streamlined shapes encounter less air resistance and, therefore, go faster.

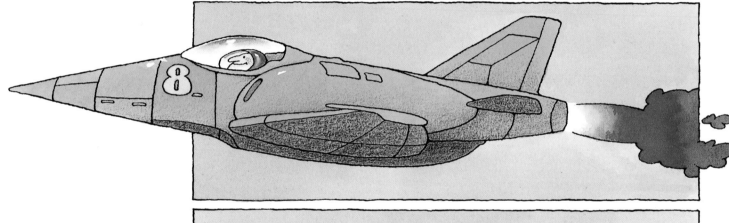

There is no air resistance in space because there is no air.
Spaceships can be any shape and still move very fast!

Draw your own spaceship.

Bigger and Better?

This is a big spaceship.   This is a bigger spaceship.

This is the biggest spaceship.

The Space Station

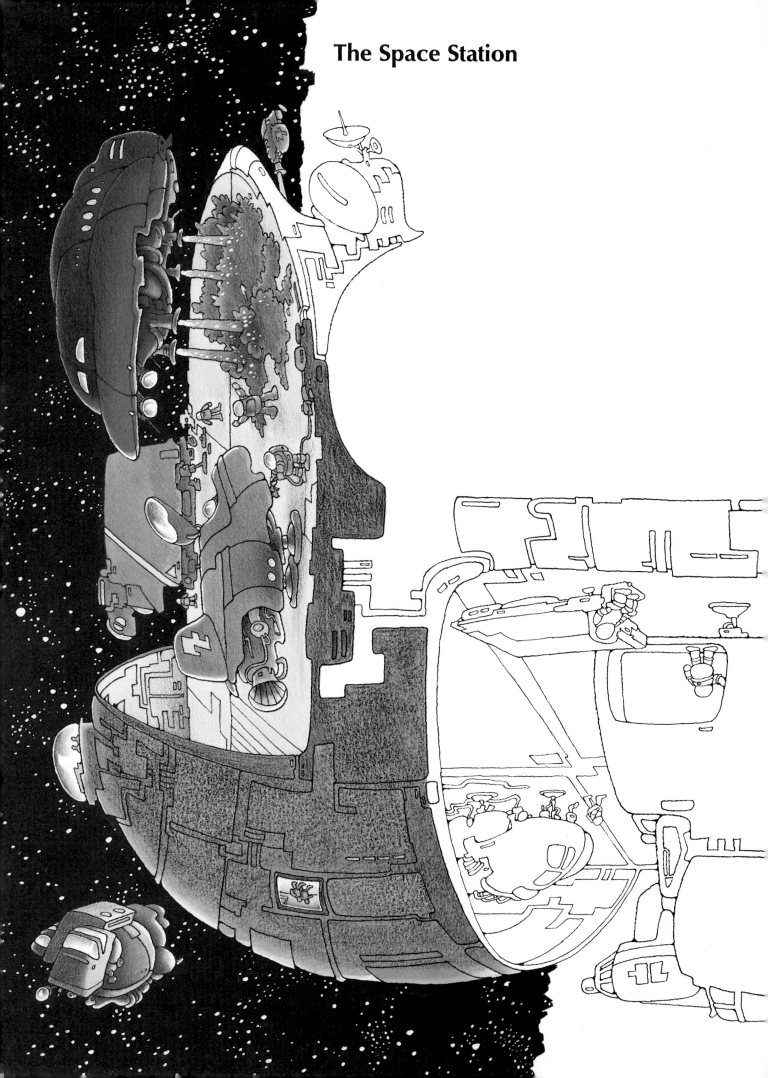

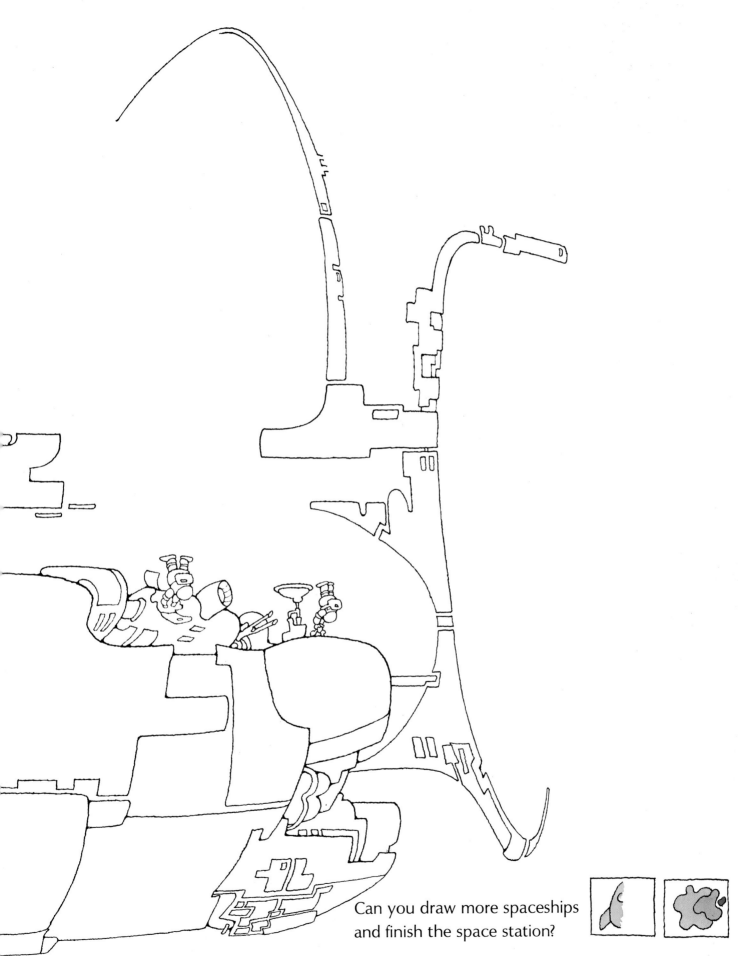

Can you draw more spaceships and finish the space station?

Crazy Creatures

These are space creatures that are very easy to draw.

Lay your hand flat on the page and trace around it.
Now add what you want to make your own alien.

15

Awful Aliens

Here are some aliens caught in time cells.

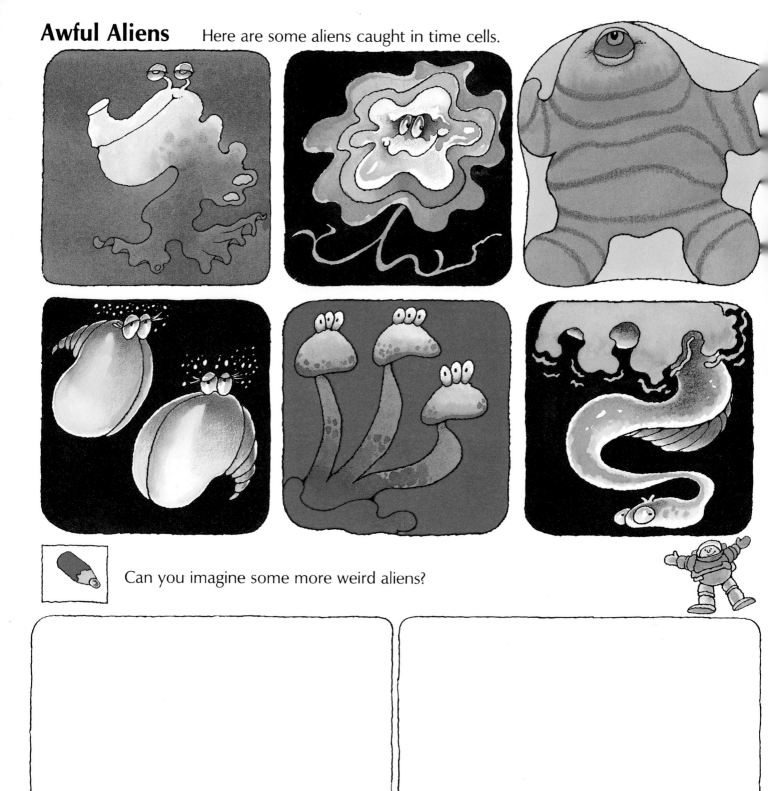

Can you imagine some more weird aliens?

These aliens have evolved from different life forms that we can recognize.
One is a Beetle-being; the other is an Astrofish.

Can you draw an alien that has evolved from a bird?
Think of a name for it.

Planet Ronng

This is a very strange planet. How many odd things can you see?

Into the Unknown

These explorers have just landed on an unknown planet far out in space.
They meet a sweet little alien but then come face-to-face with its mother!
Can you draw her?

Moon Madness

On the moon people weigh much less than they do here on earth.
They can jump much higher and slide about more.
Draw some moon explorers having fun on the moon.
Put some close to you, others in the middle, and some far away.

Aliens with Special Features

These are very advanced aliens.
One has hair that bears fruit; the other has a flute for a nose so that it can always play music.

Can you draw an alien with more than one head so that it always has someone to talk to?